SNO ELLING WITH THE SAW SHARK

DINOSAUR COVE™

DINOSAUR COVE™

SNORKELLING WITH
THE SAW SHARK

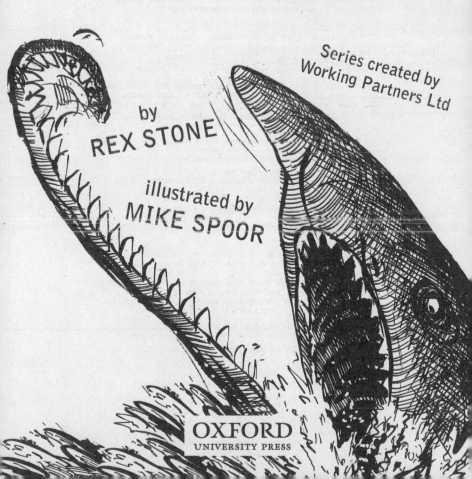

by
REX STONE

illustrated by
MIKE SPOOR

Series created by
Working Partners Ltd

OXFORD
UNIVERSITY PRESS

Special thanks to Jane Clarke

For Otto   R.S.

For Vicki, Lucie, Amber, Therese, Yan
and the Bright Bunch   M.S.

OXFORD
UNIVERSITY PRESS

Great Clarendon Street, Oxford OX2 6DP
Oxford University Press is a department of the University of Oxford.
It furthers the University's objective of excellence in research, scholarship,
and education by publishing worldwide in

Oxford   New York

Auckland   Cape Town   Dar es Salaam   Hong Kong   Karachi
Kuala Lumpur   Madrid   Melbourne   Mexico City   Nairobi
New Delhi   Shanghai   Taipei   Toronto

With offices in

Argentina   Austria   Brazil   Chile   Czech Republic   France   Greece
Guatemala   Hungary   Italy   Japan   Poland   Portugal   Singapore
South Korea   Switzerland   Thailand   Turkey   Ukraine   Vietnam

Oxford is a registered trade mark of Oxford University Press
in the UK and in certain other countries

Series created by Working Partners Ltd
Dinosaur Cove is a registered trademark of Working Partners Ltd

The moral rights of the author have been asserted

Database right Oxford University Press (maker)

First published 2012

3

British Library Cataloguing in Publication Data

Data available

ISBN: 978-0-19-275632-9

Printed in Great Britain
Paper used in the production of this book is a natural,
recyclable product made from wood grown in sustainable forests
The manufacturing process conforms to the environmental
regulations of the country of origin

FACT FILE

➡️ WHEN JAMIE AND HIS BEST FRIEND, TOM, STEP THROUGH THE FOSSILIZED PRINTS AT DINO COVE, THEY FIND THEMSELVES IN A PREHISTORIC WORLD. THE PERMIAN ERA IS A TIME EVEN BEFORE DINOSAURS, AND THEY'RE AMAZED BY THE ANCIENT CREATURES THAT LIVE IN THE PERMIAN SEAS. THE BOYS SWIM INTO A LAGOON FULL OF SAW SHARKS. BUT THE SHARKS AREN'T PLEASED TO SEE JAMIE AND TOM. CAN THE BOYS DISCOVER THE SHARKS' SECRET — AND AVOID THEIR DEADLY TEETH?

JAMIE

- **FULL NAME:** JAMIE MORGAN
- **AGE:** 8 YEARS
- **SIZE:** 1 JATOM*
- **TOP SPEED:** 10 KPH
- **LIKES:** FOSSIL HUNTING AND LEARNING ABOUT DINOSAURS
- **DISLIKES:** BEING STUCK INDOORS

Jamie's eye

Jamie's foot

Jamie's hand

*NOTE A JATOM IS THE SIZE OF JAMIE OR TOM: 125 CM TALL AND 27 KG IN WEIGHT

TOM

- **FULL NAME:** THOMAS CLAY
- **AGE:** 8 YEARS
- **SIZE:** 1 JATOM*
- **TOP SPEED:** 10 KPH
- **LIKES:** TRACKING ANIMALS AND EXPLORING WILDLIFE
- **DISLIKES:** RAINY DAYS

Tom's eye

Tom's hand

WANNA

- **FULL NAME:** WANNANOSAURUS
- **AGE:** 65–80 MILLION YEARS**
- **SIZE:** LESS THAN A JATOM*
- **TOP SPEED:** 50 KPH, ESPECIALLY WHEN BEING CHASED BY A T-REX
- **LIKES:** STINKY GINGKO FRUIT AND BANGING HIS HEAD ON TREE TRUNKS
- **DISLIKES:** SCARY DINOSAURS

Wanna's head

Wanna's foot

*NOTE: A JATOM IS THE SIZE OF JAMIE OR TOM: 125 CM TALL AND 27 KG IN WEIGHT
**NOTE: SCIENTISTS CALL THIS PERIOD THE LATE CRETACEOUS

HELICOPRION

Helicoprion's jaw

Helicoprion's teeth

Helicoprion's eye

Helicoprion's fin

- **FULL NAME:** HELICOPRION
- **AGE:** 280 MILLION YEARS***
- **HEIGHT:** HALF A JATOM*
- **LENGTH:** 2 JATOMS*
- **LIKES:** FLICKING OUT ITS JAW TO CATCH PERMIAN FISH AND SLIDING ITS TOOTHY JAW INSIDE AMMONITE SHELLS
- **DISLIKES:** ANYONE SWIMMING NEAR ITS YOUNG

*NOTE: A JATOM IS THE SIZE OF JAMIE OR TOM: 125 CM TALL AND 27 KG IN WEIGHT
***NOTE: SCIENTISTS CALL THIS PERIOD THE PERMIAN

DINOSAUR COVE

Village

Marina

Sealight Head

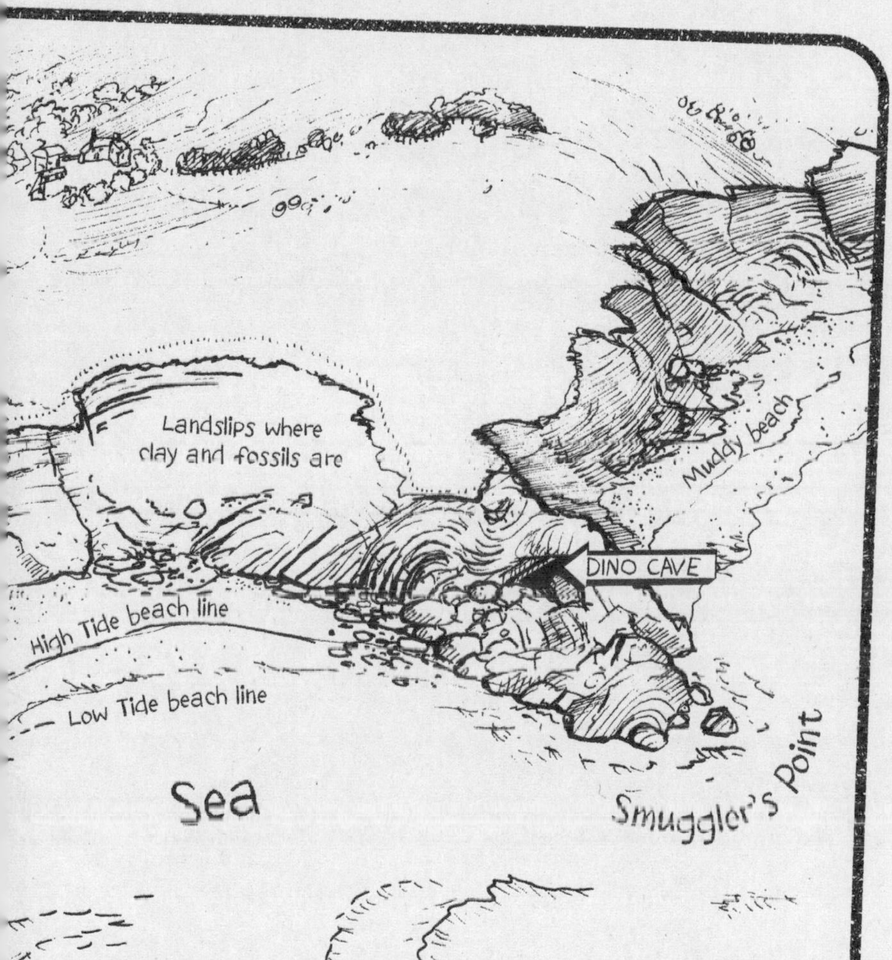

Landslips where clay and fossils are

Muddy beach

DINO CAVE

High Tide beach line

Low Tide beach line

Sea

Smuggler's Point

CHAPTER 1

Jamie Morgan ripped off his diver's mask and snorkel.

'Look what I found!' he yelled, splashing out of the chilly waves. He raced up the beach at Dinosaur Cove, dragging what looked like a clump of writhing green tentacles behind him.

'A seaweed-o-saurus?' laughed Tom Clay, Jamie's best friend. Tom was standing in a big rockpool, with his mask and snorkel pushed up on top of his head. He carefully put a cone-shaped seashell into a bucket

on the edge of the pool and
clambered out to take a look.

Tucked among the seaweed
was a brown, transparent pouch.
Inside it wriggled a small fish
with a triangular fin on its back.
'Cool!' Tom declared. 'But
what is it?'

The boys waved to Jamie's
grandad. He slung his bag of
fishing equipment over his
shoulder and came to join them.

'A mermaid's purse!' Grandad
exclaimed. 'You don't
often see one with a
live dogfish in it.'

'Maybe it's
the mermaid's
pet,' Jamie
joked.

'Mermaid's purse is the common name for
the egg case of a dogfish,' Grandad explained.
'It's a kind of little shark. This one will grow
about as long as your forearm.'

'I'll put it back into the water so it can
hatch.' Jamie put the seaweed into the rock
pool. 'What's in the bucket, Tom?'

'Hermit crabs.' Tom gently tipped out
five different-shaped seashells that the crabs
were using as homes. One by one, each shell
sprouted pincers and a pair of googly eyes on

stalks. The hermit crabs scuttled off
sideways and hid amongst the
rocks and seaweed.

'Time I was off
home, too,' Grandad
said, looking at his watch. 'Feed the fish with
the rest of this bait—they love it!' He handed
Jamie a couple of small bags of the incredibly
smelly crumbly cheese he usually put in their
cheese and pickle sandwiches. As Grandad
climbed the path back up to the lighthouse,
he called over his shoulder, 'Let me know how
you get on road-testing my new drybag . . .'

A grey cloud crossed the early summer sun
and Jamie shivered. He looked around for
his backpack. He'd put it inside Grandad's
drybag—a bright yellow, waterproof bag—

down on the shoreline. When he saw it he let out a gasp. 'Oh no!'

The waves were breaking over the drybag and it was about to float away on the high tide. Jamie dashed down and grabbed it by the shoulder strap, just in time to stop it being washed out to sea. The outside of the drybag was dripping wet, but when he unclipped the fastener and unrolled the top, his backpack was safe and dry inside.

'This drybag really works!' he exclaimed, handing Tom his T-shirt and putting on his own. He stuffed the cheese bait into the backpack and re-sealed everything in the drybag.

'Let's take a closer look in the rock pool.' Tom pulled his mask and snorkel down over his eyes and mouth and

lay on his tummy with his head in the pool.
Jamie did the same.

A shoal of shrimps with ten legs and see-
through armour plating drifted in with the
tide, waving their feelers. One tiny shrimp
blundered into the path of a sea anemone
that looked like a bright red daisy. It grabbed
the shrimp in its tentacles.

Jamie nudged Tom and they raised their
heads above the surface. 'There's a whole

universe of predators and prey down there—a bit like Dino World!' Jamie remarked, thinking of the amazing secret world he and Tom had discovered in the Cove. They'd had some awesome adventures there, most recently exploring the Permian era—which was 265 million years ago!

'Some of those creatures in the rock pool even look prehistoric,' Tom said, sitting up and rubbing the goose pimples on his arm. 'Like you!'

Jamie dipped his snorkel into the cold sea water then blew it all over his friend. 'The Permian sea would be a lot warmer than this,' he chuckled as Tom shrieked and jumped to his feet.

'So let's check out the sea life in the Permian!' Tom exclaimed. 'The Fossil Finder, binoculars, and

Permian trilobite are already in the backpack, aren't they?'

'Check!' Jamie grabbed Grandad's dry bag and the boys scrambled up the rocks to Smuggler's Point. In no time at all, they were fitting their feet into the fossilized dinosaur footprints that led across the floor of their secret cave. There was a dazzling flash, and the soles of the boys' rubber water shoes scrunched in the fresh dino footprints on the sandy floor of a warm dark tunnel. They were back in the Permian!

Jamie's body tingled with
excitement as he led the
way to the surface, the
hot air like a hairdryer
on his chilly damp
T-shirt. The boys
crawled out
into the

clump of ferns that concealed the entrance to the tunnel. There was a sudden high-pitched whine and the sky darkened. They ducked down as a cloud of insects whirred past.

'Weird—they look like shrimps with wings!' said Jamie. 'Wonder what they taste like?'

'Somewhere out there, there's a predator wondering what we taste like. We're in inostrancevia territory, remember?' Tom rummaged in Jamie's backpack for his binoculars, hooked the cord over his neck, and scanned the rocky red mountainside above the tunnel entrance. There was no sign of the bear-like beast, with its long reptilian tail and vicious fangs, which seemed to appear whenever the boys arrived in the Permian.

'Phew,' said Tom. He pulled the binoculars up over his head, to pass them to Jamie, but the cord twanged off his mask and snorkel, which tumbled back down the tunnel. 'Whoops! I'll go back and get 'em.'

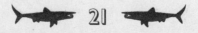

Tom
handed the
binoculars to
Jamie and dropped
down the tunnel. Jamie
focused them on one of the
shrimp-like insects, which had landed on
a fern in front of him. It looked fearsome, but
he couldn't see a sting.

All of a sudden, both
lenses of the binoculars

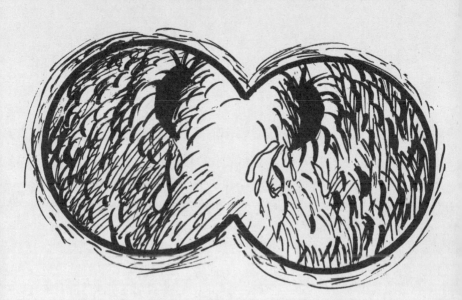

went dark. Jamie blinked and re-focused.
He could make out what seemed to be two
tunnels, with a string of snot dripping from
one of them. He was looking up the nose of a
giant reptile!

Jamie's stomach did a somersault.

Snurfff!

The beast snorted, clouding the lenses.

'Help!' Jamie yelled, hurling the binoculars
at the creature.

CHAPTER 2

The binocular cord caught on the end of a scaly wannanosaurus nose. It was Wanna, the two-legged dinosaur from the Cretaceous, who accompanied the boys on all their adventures.

Gak, gak, gak!

Wanna bobbed his head up and down in alarm. Jamie caught the binoculars as the little dino shook them off his nose.

Tom re-emerged from the tunnel with his mask and snorkel perched on top of his head.

'What's all the fuss about?' Tom asked.

Gak-ak-ak-ak-ak!

Wanna's eyes opened wide in alarm. Jamie followed the dinosaur's gaze.

The snorkel made Tom look as if he had a horn growing out of his head and the sun was shining off the mask like a fiery third eye.

Gak-ak-ak-ak-ak!

Wanna gakked as fast as a round of gunfire, lowered his bony head and began to claw at the ground.

'I don't think he recognizes us in our diving gear,' Jamie hissed. 'He's revving up to charge . . . '

'It's only us, Wanna,' Tom said soothingly. 'We're your friends!'

At the sound of Tom's voice, Wanna stopped clawing the ground. He sniffed the air suspiciously.

26

'I know what will convince him,' Jamie
said, unrolling the top of the drybag. He
stuffed the binoculars into his backpack
and took out one of Grandad's bags of
stinky cheese bait. He opened it up. Wanna
stretched out his neck and snuffled at it.

T'choo!

The little dino sneezed. His tail began to
wag and he scampered up
to the boys, grunking
happily. Jamie tied up
the top of the cheese
bag and stuffed it
into the pocket of his
swimming trunks.

'Clever Wanna,'
Tom laughed, as they
both scratched the dino
on his scaly nose. 'The
cheese is so smelly, he

recognized it even though
it wasn't in a sandwich
with pickle!'

They set off towards the
shore. Jamie led the way
across the sizzling plains,
skirting the red sand dunes
and keeping an eye open
for the inostie. Soon, they
could see glimpses of blue
sea beyond the dunes.

Suddenly, Tom put
his finger to his lips and
pointed. Between them and
the sparkling water was a
herd of monstrous lizards
with crocodile-like jaws.
The creatures were ripping
into a carcass. They raised
and lowered the red-orange,

crescent-shaped sails on their backs and hissed
at each other as they squabbled over the
tastiest parts of their rotting food.

'Dimetrodon,' Jamie said. 'They're awesome,
but their dinner sure does stink!' He held his
nose as they crept past.

One of the dimies stopped chewing for
a moment. A lump of meat fell from its
jaws and it looked around, its gleaming eyes

scanning the plains.
The dimie's nostrils
flared as it sniffed
loudly.

'Uh-oh,'
muttered Tom.
'It thinks it can
smell dessert.'

'And that's us,'
added Jamie with a gulp.

GEE OW-OW-OW!

The dimie screeched as it lunged towards
the boys and Wanna. Jamie grabbed their
dino friend and they all piled behind a tall
sand dune. After a few moments, Tom peered
over the top of it.

'It's gone back to the herd,' he said with a
relieved grin.

They continued their way to the shore.
Ahead, the sand dunes flattened into a sandy

red beach at the edge of the Permian ocean. Right by their feet, the sand was scored with a long narrow line that led down to the sea.

'What made that track?' Tom murmured.

A slight movement near the edge of the water caught Jamie's eye. 'That did!' he exclaimed.

The boys raced down the beach just in time to see a brown, snake-like creature, as long as a baseball bat, crawl into the sea on its four tiny legs.

Tom dug out the Fossil Finder from the backpack and switched it on. The *HAPPY HUNTING* screen popped up and Tom typed in '*PERMIAN SNAKE-LIKE LIZARD*'. A picture of the creature they'd seen appeared.

'RH-YN-CH-ON-KOS,' Tom read aloud. '**AN AMPHIBIAN LIKE A GIANT NEWT OR SALAMANDER THAT CAN LIVE ON THE LAND OR IN THE WATER.**'

'Cool!' Jamie said, stowing the Fossil Finder back inside the backpack once more and re-fastening the drybag. 'Let's go snorkelling.' He pointed to a rocky headland that sloped down into the sea. 'That looks like the perfect place.'

The boys and Wanna hurried towards it.

'Hey, take a look at this!' yelled Tom.

He raced up to a huge trilobite shell lying
at the foot of the headland. It was the length
of Tom's arm-span and looked like a gigantic
woodlouse, with its body divided into ribbed
sections. But it was empty, and so were the
short legs that dangled like a fringe around it.

'Trilobites shed their shells
when they grew out of them,'
Tom murmured. 'It must be
even bigger now!'

Wanna sniffed curiously at the moulted shell, then hopped inside. He wriggled about so that his tail and rear legs were sticking out of the back of the shell. 'He looks like one of those hermit crabs you found in the rock pool!' Jamie laughed.

Grunk!

Wanna's voice echoed inside the shell. The empty trilobite shook as the little dino seemed to try to climb out.

GRUNK!

'The hermit trilo-wanna-saur's stuck!' Tom chortled. 'Rescue him!'

Jamie and Tom each took hold of one of Wanna's legs. There was a crackling noise and then a loud pop as the shell

cracked in two and Wanna burst out. One
half of the shell still had the trilobite's empty
legs attached, while the other was like an
enormous shiny bowl.

'Come on, let's get in the water,' Jamie said.

'Wanna had better stay here,' said Tom,
remembering their adventure in the Jurassic
ocean. 'He's not much good at swimming.' He
turned to Jamie. 'Last one in's a bone-head!'

The boys took off their t-shirts and put
them into the backpack. Pulling down their
masks and snorkels, they raced into the sea.

'Wow!' Jamie yelled. 'It's like a warm salty bath.'

They swam a few strokes and looked back to the shore. Wanna was standing beside the pieces of trilobite shell, grunking unhappily.

'I don't think he likes being left behind,' said Tom.

Jamie looked at the pieces of shell. 'He doesn't have to be. He's standing next to a prehistoric boat!'

'So he is,' Tom laughed.

They splashed out of the water and raced up to the broken trilobite shell. Jamie put the

drybag inside the half without
the legs attached and Wanna
hopped in next to it.

'We're launching you, Wanna!'
Jamie announced. 'You'll love it!'

Wanna grunked nervously as
they pushed the shell onto the water.
It wobbled precariously for a moment,
then steadied. Their dino friend looked
around happily as the boys towed his
trilobite boat out along the edge of
the rocky headland.

'Snorkel time!' said Jamie, and
floated face down. Beneath him, seaweed
swirled around rocks and corals that were
colours of the rainbow. It was an underwater
jungle.

He resurfaced next to Tom.

'We've got a whole new world to explore,'
Jamie gasped. 'Awesome!'

CHAPTER 3

Jamie dipped his face below the surface of the water and gazed down on a forest of red, orange, and purple corals. The rocks were covered in pink anemones the size of footballs. One put out its tentacles and snatched at his feet.

Lucky I'm too big for it to grab! Jamie thought.

He followed Tom into a sheltered lagoon, pushing Wanna's shell-boat. A cluster of sea creatures in wheel-like shells hung in the

water, slowly
moving up and
down like yo-yos on
strings. Some were tiny,
but others were as big as
the boys. Jamie recognized
them from the fossils in his
dad's Dinosaur Museum.

He poked his head above
the surface.

'Live ammonites!' he exclaimed.

Tom gestured to the seabed. A line of
trilobites was trundling between the rocks
and corals like a troupe of giant underwater
woodlice, heading towards a crevice between
the rocks. Jamie pushed Wanna's boat through,
into a half-submerged cavern. There was
hardly any light and the water was a deep, dark
blue. The seabed was studded with fluorescent
green stars like the world was upside down.

Tom surfaced next to him.

'Now those really are starfish!' Tom spluttered, spitting water out of his mouth. 'They're giving off light like deep sea creatures.'

'You'd never know that from their fossils!' Jamie looked round the spooky cave. 'Hey! Where's Wanna off to?'

Wanna's trilobite boat drifted through a small opening at the opposite end of the cavern.

'There must be another cave through there,' Tom said. 'Let's check it out!'

Gak . . . gak . . . gak . . .

Wanna's alarm call echoed through the hole, followed by loud panicky splashing.

Tom and Jamie

looked at each other, then dived
into the cave. It was a smaller
than the starfish
cave, but not
as dark. Rays of sunlight were
filtering through leafy vines that
hung down over the deep
blue water from a big
hole in the roof. The air was
as hot and humid as a sauna.

Wanna was in the middle of the cave,
clutching onto the floating yellow drybag.

'He's capsized his shell-boat,' Jamie laughed,
starting to swim out to drag Wanna back.

But Tom grabbed him by the ankle.

'Stop!' Tom yelled. He pointed to
something in the water.

Jamie's blood ran cold. Three triangular
fins were circling Wanna's drybag float. That
could only mean one thing . . .

'Sharks!' he gasped.

The boys ducked beneath the surface and stared through their masks. The torpedo-shaped sharks were dappled blue and grey, making them hard to see in the shadow-flecked sea.

'They're much bigger than we are,' Jamie said when they'd resurfaced. 'We've got to get Wanna out of the water!'

With a rush of spray, one of the sharks threw itself out of the water, its jaws open

wide. It looked as if it had a circular saw in
its mouth.

'Aaargh!' the boys yelled together in fright.
Wanna's terrified gaks echoed round the cave.

'Did you see its teeth?' Jamie gasped.
'They're in a spiral!'

'Weird! Hey, maybe Wanna can climb
onto this.' Tom reached for a gigantic
thick rubbery leaf, which was
attached to a vine that
hung from

the roof of the
cave. His hand
was shaking but he got hold
of it. 'Let's hope Wanna
knows how to surf,' he
murmured.

He yanked the
leaf free and pushed
it towards their
floundering friend.

S . . . s . . . s . . . *nap!*

The shark shot its saw-like teeth
out of its bottom jaw, so they were as
straight and sharp as a sword. It shredded
the leaf, splattering bits of green on the boys'
masks. Then the shark's teeth curled back
into its spiral jaw. It flicked its tail and turned
in the water.

'It's coming for us!' Tom shrieked.

CHAPTER 4

The shark powered across the cave. It swam
just beneath the surface, its body gleaming
like a submarine. Once more it unfurled
its jagged teeth. Then it swerved, carving
through the water towards Tom.

'Look out!' Jamie yelled.

The shark raised its saw of teeth out of
the water and swept it from side to side in
a slicing motion. Tom kicked out and rolled
away from the creature's path. It shot past
them, its pale eyes rolled back with anger.

The shark plunged back underwater and twisted round to face the boys again.

Tom spat out a mouthful of seawater. 'It's launching another attack!'

The boys backed away from the approaching shark.

Clunk!

Jamie's head hit something sticking out from the cavern wall. It was a rocky ledge, just above the water! It ran round the cavern, sloping upwards towards the opposite side.

'Get out of the water!' he yelled.

Just in time, Jamie and Tom hauled themselves onto the ledge. The shark snapped its spiral jaws again, and with another flick of its tail sped back towards Wanna.

Gak!

Wanna's legs splashed wildly. The shark's teeth caught the corner of the yellow drybag and the cave echoed with a hissing noise.

Gak!

'The bag's been punctured,' Jamie groaned. 'It'll sink. The Fossil Finder will be ruined—and Wanna will be shark bait!'

Then he remembered something.

'Fish bait!' Jamie pulled the bag of Grandad's stinky cheese out of his pocket and ran up the sloping ledge, as far away from Wanna as he could. 'Here's hoping dino sharks like this,' he muttered, sprinkling the smelly cheese into the water.

The sharks stopped circling and swam straight towards the cheese. The sea boiled as they twisted and turned, shooting out their strange jaws to try to get hold of the tiny pieces.

'Swim, Wanna!' Tom yelled, jumping up and down and waving his arms. 'Swim!' Wanna was hanging on to the drybag, desperately kicking his feet. But it was no good. The bag was going under—and so was Wanna!

CHAPTER 5

Jamie hurled himself onto one of the rope-like vines that dangled down from the hole in the cave roof.

'Yee-ha!' he yelled, sticking out his feet as he swung across the surface of the water.

Thunk!

His feet connected with Wanna's back and propelled the little dino and his float towards Tom.

Tom reached out and managed to catch hold of the corner of the bag. 'Got it!' he

yelled triumphantly. 'Help me haul Wanna in.'

Jamie kicked his legs and swung himself back onto the ledge. He let go of the vine and knelt down to grab one of Wanna's scaly legs. Together the boys hauled their dino friend to safety. Wanna lay on the ledge, soaking wet and grunking in relief.

Jamie dragged the dripping yellow drybag up beside them.

Yee-ha!

'Is the Fossil Finder OK?' Tom asked anxiously, looking at the hole in the corner of the bag.

Jamie rolled down the top of the drybag and took out the backpack.

'The outside's a bit damp,' he murmured, 'but it's dry inside.' He pulled out the Fossil Finder and opened it up. The *HAPPY HUNTING* screen appeared at once.

'It's still working,' he grinned. He typed '*SPIRAL SAW SHARK*' into the search box and the name '*HELICOPRION*' flashed up. '*HELLY-COP-REE-ON,*' he read. 'It says they lived mostly on small fish and shelled sea creatures. The spiral of teeth was perfect for getting into ammonite shells.' He stashed the Fossil Finder and the yellow drybag inside his backpack. 'So why did they attack Wanna?'

'This is a case for Tom Clay, wildlife reporter,' Tom declared, walking round the ledge and talking into his snorkel as if it was a microphone. 'Today, for the very first time, we're in the Permian watching the feeding frenzy of the mysterious spiral saw shark, helicoprion,' he commented to his imaginary audience. 'Why have these strange shell-crunchers turned into Wanna-hunters? Perhaps their behaviour will give us a clue . . . '

Tom stopped at the highest point of the ledge, above the still-feasting sharks. He pushed his snorkel microphone away from his mouth.

'I've found eight clues!' he yelled.

'What do you mean?' Jamie asked. He and Wanna hurried to

join him. They peered down cautiously into the water.

Eight baby sharks, each the size of a dogfish, had joined the three big helicoprion and were fighting over the remaining traces of cheese. The boys and Wanna watched, fascinated, as the little sharks shot out their spiral saws, then coiled them back into their mouths.

'We're in a shark nursery!' Tom said. 'I reckon the hellies attacked Wanna because they thought he was a predator coming to eat their young.'

'Makes sense—but they'll think we're predators too if we hang around too long,' Jamie pointed out. 'Let's swim for it while there's some cheese left.' He looked around in alarm. 'Where's the entrance to the cave gone?'

Water was lapping over the lowest part of the ledge.

'The tide's come in and covered it!' Tom groaned. 'We're stuck! We'll never get Wanna to swim underwater.'

'Don't panic, bonehead.' Jamie grabbed the end of one of the vines hanging through the hole in the cave roof.

'We can climb out and haul Wanna up after us.'

'Ace!' Tom grabbed a pair of vines and tied them around Wanna, hooking them under his armpits like a parachute harness.

Then he took hold of
a vine himself.

Hand over hand,
the boys began to
climb up towards the
hole in the roof, using
their rubber water
shoes to grip the vine
with their feet.

'This is hard
work!' Jamie gasped.
He glanced down
on the scene below.
The hellies must
have eaten all the
cheese because they
were rushing at the
ledge with open jaws.
Wanna was leaping
from foot to foot to

avoid them. There
was no time to lose!
The boys scrambled out
onto the rocky vine-draped
headland. They grabbed hold of
the vines that were tied to Wanna
and braced themselves against the rocks.
'One, two, three . . . heave!' Jamie ordered.
Through the hole, they could see Wanna
slowly getting bigger as he rose above
the water, grunking nervously.

'It's working!' Tom puffed. But
the instant the words were out of his
mouth, there was a loud crack.

Inside the cave, Wanna was swinging from
side to side, gakking wildly and flailing his legs.
The prehistoric sharks leapt out of the water,
trying to reach him with their sharp toothy saws.

'One of the vines has snapped!' Jamie
groaned. 'The hellies are going to get him!'

CHAPTER 6

'Pull him up, quick!' Tom yelled.

But Wanna's weight made the remaining vine stretch like a bungee rope. He gave a terrified *grunk* as he bounced up and down above the circling sharks. The centre of the vine was fraying, green tendrils plopping into the water.

'This vine's going to break soon, as well,' gasped Jamie. 'We haven't got long!'

One of the sharks sprang from the water, its saw slicing just past Wanna.

'One, two, three . . .
heave!' cried Tom.

They yanked desperately on the
remaining vine until Wanna's bony
head emerged through the hole.
The vine finally tore in two,
but Jamie just managed to
grab one of Wanna's front
legs. Together, he and
Tom hauled him out
onto the rocky
headland.

Heave!

Wanna wagged his tail and grunked for joy.

'Go, dino team!' Tom and Jamie yelled, giving each other a high five.

'My hands are all wrinkly from being underwater,' Jamie remarked, examining his crinkled fingertips.

'So are mine,' Tom said. He untied the vines from Wanna. 'Wanna's scales are soggy, too. I reckon it's time we went back. If we stay any longer, we'll turn into prunes!'

They clambered over the rocky headland
into a sheltered patch of Permian forest,
where conifer trees and thick bushy ferns grew
between the rocks.

Wanna put his head on one side.

'He's heard something.' Tom said nervously.

Grrr . . . arrr!

The boys looked at one another. That roar
was unmistakeable. The inostrancevia was
looking for dinner—and they were on the
menu again!

Grrr ... arrr!

'It must have tracked us to the beach,' Jamie muttered, 'then heard us pulling Wanna out.'

Garr!

The roar sounded closer now and was followed by a loud snuffle. Wanna hopped uncomfortably from foot to foot.

'It's sniffing us out,' Tom groaned. 'We need to put if off our scent.'

'Stinky cheese!' cried Jamie. 'Grandad gave us two bags of it, remember? Maybe the inostie will go for the cheese rather than us.'

He delved into his backpack
and opened the bag. The cheese
had ripened in the heat and stank like
hundred-year-old sweaty football boots.

Tom held his nose. 'That might just do it!'
he gagged.

Somewhere nearby, the inostie growled
again.

Jamie quickly sprinkled the cheese on the
ground. Then the boys and Wanna flattened
their backs against a thick conifer trunk.

A smell like hot dung filled the air.
Jamie peered out from behind the tree.
A bear-sized creature with enormous sabre-
like canine teeth and mangy red-brown
fur lumbered out of the ferns. It stopped
in its tracks and sniffed. Then it swished
its long scaly tail and put its nose to the
ground. The boys were so close they could
see the creature's long blue tongue flickering

70

out as it slurped up the
crumbs of cheese.

'It's going mad for it!' Jamie
whispered. 'Quick, let's sneak
away . . .'

Jamie, Tom, and Wanna
crept through the
forest under cover
of the ferns, then
scrambled down
the rocky

headland to the beach.
They passed a pile of
stripped bones that
were the remains of the
dimetrodons' dinner,
and soon they arrived
back at the entrance
to the secret cave.
Wanna wagged his tail
and dropped down into
the tunnel. The boys
followed.

'I think he wants
to get as far away from
Permian sharks as he
can!' Tom joked.

'Bye, Wanna!' they
both called as their dino
friend disappeared into
the darkness.

Jamie and Tom stepped backwards into the fresh sandy footprints that led across the floor of the underground cave.

In a flash, they were back in the secret cave on Smuggler's Point.

'It's freezing compared to the Permian!' Tom shivered as they emerged onto the headland above Dinosaur Cove. The sky was cloudy and the sea looked grey.

Tom rummaged in the drybag for his binoculars.

'It only just survived its test run!' he commented.

Jamie was staring into the distance with his mouth open. 'Is that what I think it is?' He pointed out to sea. A triangular fin was slicing through the water.

Tom checked it out with his binoculars. 'It's as big as the hellies!' he exclaimed. 'It must be a basking shark. I've heard they

sometimes visit the Cove in the summer, but this is the first time I've ever seen one! They're plankton eaters.'

'Huge, but harmless,' Jamie grinned as he took his turn with the binoculars. He could see the dappled body of the shark and its great gaping mouth just beneath the surface. 'Now, that's the sort of shark I like!'

GLOSSARY

Ammonite (am-on-ite) – an extinct animal with octopus-like legs and often a spiral-shaped shell that lived in the ocean.

Dimetrodon (dy-mee-tr-oh-don) – a sail-backed, mammal-like reptile.

Helicoprion (hel-ik-oh-pree-on) – a carnivorous shark that had teeth arranged on a spiral-shaped jaw.

Hermit crab – a type of crab without its own shell, which moves into empty shells and carries them around to protect itself from predators.

Inostrancevia (in-os-tran-see-vee-ah) – a large, predatory mammal-like reptile.

Permian (per-mee-an) – from about 250 to 300 million years ago, when the earth was divided into one big mass of land and an enormous ocean. Dinosaurs did not yet exist and roaches were the dominant species.

Pangaea (pan-jee-ah) – a single continent that existed about 250 million years ago before the continents were separated into their current configuration.

Rhynchonkos (rin-kon-kos) – a long, thin amphibian which looked like a giant newt and could live on the water or dry land.

Sea anemone (see an-em-on-nee) – a stationary animal often attached to rocks or to the sea bed. It has many tentacles and may eat small fish.

Shrimp – a shelled crustacean which lives in fresh or salt water.

Trilobite (try-loh-byt) – an extinct marine animal that had an outside skeleton divided into three parts.

Wannanosaurus (wah-nan-oh-sor-us) – a dinosaur that only ate plants and used its hard, flat skull to defend itself. Named after the place it was discovered: Wannano in China.

We're heading your way ...
and there's millions of us